The Sierra Club, founded in 1892 by John Muir, has devoted itself to the study and protection of the earth's scenic and ecological resources — mountains, wetlands, woodlands, wild shores and rivers, deserts and plains. The publishing program of the Sierra Club offers books to the public as a nonprofit educational service in the hope that they may enlarge the public's understanding of the Club's basic concerns. The Sierra Club has some sixty chapters in the United States and in Canada. For information about how you may participate in its programs to preserve wilderness and the quality of life, please address inquiries to Sierra Club, 730 Polk Street, San Francisco, CA 94109.

First edition

Library of Congress Cataloging-in-Publication Data

Sackett, Elisabeth.
    Danger on the Arctic ice/Elisabeth Sackett: illustrations by
Martin Camm. — 1st ed.
        p.   cm.
    Summary: As summer brings more activity to the Arctic, a harp seal
pup encounters danger from both animal and human hunters.
    ISBN 0-316-76598-8
    1. Harp seal — Juvenile fiction. [1. Harp seal — Fiction. 2. Seal
(Animals) — Fiction.] I. Camm, Martin, ill. II. Title.
PZ10.3.S127Dan   1990
[E] — dc20   90-53671

Sierra Club Books/Little, Brown children's books are published by
Little, Brown and Company (Inc.) in association with Sierra Club Books.

10   9   8   7   6   5   4   3   2   1

Published simultaneously in Canada by
Little, Brown & Company (Canada) Limited

Printed in Spain

DEP. LEG. B-19.646-91

Danger on the Arctic Ice

by Elisabeth Sackett

Illustrations by Martin Camm

Introduction by Cynthia Overbeck Bix

Sierra Club Books | Little, Brown and Company
San Francisco | Boston · Toronto · London

Introduction

At the very top of the world lies a region of snow-covered lands and icy waters called the Arctic Circle. Every spring, when the thick sea ice breaks up into floating islands, or floes, thousands of harp seals gather in the Arctic Ocean. These sleek mammals are perfectly made for their life in the sea. Their strong flippers propel them easily through the water as they hunt for fish. To keep warm, they have a special layer of fat, called blubber, and a coat of thick fur.

A harp seal baby, or pup, has big, dark eyes and a little whiskered face. Its fur is pure, snowy white. Little pups like the one in this story face many dangers. Often their mothers must leave them alone on the ice to go hunting for food. Then the pups may be attacked by animals such as the polar bear. The pups have also been in danger from human beings. For centuries, hunters clubbed the poor pups to death just to get their beautiful fur, which could be sold for high prices to people who wanted to make coats and other garments. So many pups were killed that some people began to worry that soon there would not be any harp seals left.

Starting in the 1950s, conservation and humanitarian groups began to tell the public about the cruel killing of harp seal pups. Many people stopped buying the fur, and by 1987 The United States, Canada, and the European nations had agreed to outlaw the killing.

Today seal pups are safe from human violence in most areas. But this story reminds us how important it is to continue protecting the pups, and to make sure that seals and other animals can continue to live their lives undisturbed in the snowy northern lands and seas of the Arctic Circle.

The Arctic lands had been dark and silent throughout the long winter months. The sun had not been seen in this vast, icy region; only the flickering aurora borealis lit the sky, shedding its ghostly light onto the whiteness below.

At last a faint pink glow appeared in the south. It grew slowly stronger until a red disk rose, huge and bright, above the sea. It climbed high into the sky to shine throughout the short summer.

An Arctic fox opened his eyes and blinked. He pushed his head out of the crevice in the rocks where he had been sleeping. The sunshine felt warm and welcoming, and he climbed out onto the ice pack where he stood bathed in the bright light. Around him, he heard loud cracks and booms as the ice broke and splintered in the warmth of the sun.

The Arctic fox felt tremors beneath his feet and began leaping over the ice to reach firmer ground. He did not want to float off into the great icy ocean. Now that the summer was coming, he would journey south to the tundra, where there was plenty of food.

As he made his way over the ice, the fox nearly jumped onto a small animal lying on its side, its front flippers folded over its very round body. The fox paused for a moment, sniffing at the creature, and then scampered away. His thoughts were of fat, succulent lemmings; he was not interested in seal pups.

The seal pup turned his head and watched the fox disappear over the ice. He was waiting for his mother, who was swimming in the sea in search of fish.

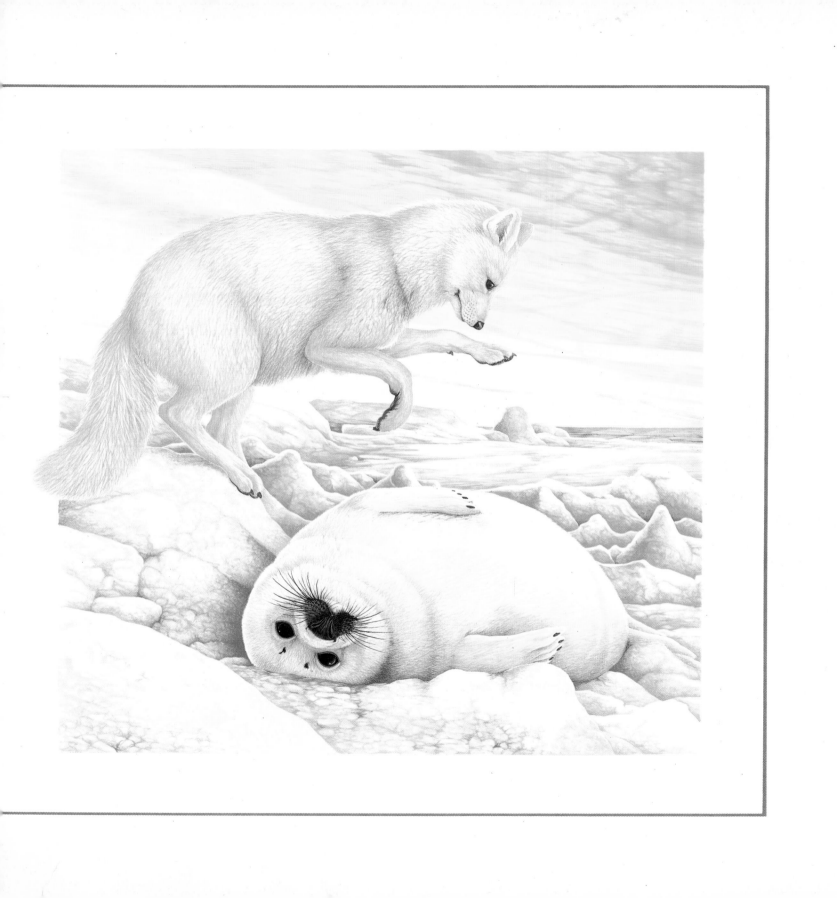

The seal pup was not yet able to hunt with his mother. He could swim a little but had not yet learned how to breathe properly under water. Also, his flippers did not seem to move together, which meant that he went around and around instead of forward. Waiting alone now on the ice, he bleated loudly, but as no one answered, he closed his eyes and soon went to sleep.

The mother seal looked for fish in the deep, dark waters. She moved quickly, her powerful front flippers thrusting her forward. She saw the silver gleam of a fish and, twisting deftly, caught the fish in her sharp teeth.

When she rose to the surface, she saw an ominous gray shape in the distance. It was a boat – and the mother seal knew it could mean trouble. Boats often carried humans who, with clubs and rifles, killed seal pups for their thick, glossy fur. She turned and swam toward the ice where her pup was waiting, sleeping peacefully.

Many animals had awoken in the warmth of the summer sun, and the Arctic lands were filled with life once again. A polar bear climbed out of an ice cave followed by her two young ones. The cubs slid and slithered along behind their mother as she led them toward the water's edge in search of food.

The seal pup awoke with a start as other seals all around him flopped into the water. They had seen the great, lumbering polar bear making her way toward them. The polar bear had noticed the seal pup lying alone and now reared up above him, raising her great arms, ready to strike.

Suddenly, the ice beneath the pup cracked and broke away. The little seal floated out into the ocean, leaving the polar bear perched on the sea's edge, very cross and very hungry.

The pup bobbed along on the water, bleating for his mother. Great seabirds flew over him, their sharp beaks gleaming.

The seal pup bleated louder and louder and beat his front flippers against the ice. Just then, a shadow fell over the sea and the little pup's iceberg bumped against something hard. He had hit the fur hunters' boat. Above him, a figure climbed quickly down a rope ladder, a long wooden club in his hand.

At that moment the little pup was pushed from behind into the sea. His mother had heard his call and had found him just in time. He sank downward, choking on the icy salt water. He felt his mother beneath him, pushing him up toward the surface. Gasping for breath, he moved his flippers in an effort to swim. His mother stayed beside him, helping him to keep above the waves, nudging him away from the boat.

They swam on until the seal pup, exhausted, began to sink again. His mother looked out above the water. Through the mist that was forming, she could make out sea spray where the ocean was beating against sharp reefs. Behind the reefs were sloping shelves of rock, climbing between steep cliffs. They would be safe there.

The mother seal swam between the reefs and pushed the limp body of her pup onto the rock shelf. She cried shrilly and put her flipper over him. For a long time he lay without moving. Then he spluttered, spat out some sea water, and opened his large, brown eyes. He bleated faintly and turned against his mother's warm side.

The Arctic sun glimmered through the mist, and waves broke against the rocks, sending droplets of water over the little pup and his mother. The two slept peacefully, knowing that they were safe and that neither polar bears nor humans would find them on this small, rocky island at the edge of the world.